The Three Bears

Byron Barton

HarperCollins*Publishers*

The Three Bears. Copyright © 1991 by Byron Barton. Printed in the U.S.A. All rights reserved. Library of Congress Cataloging-in-Publication Data. Barton, Byron. The three bears / Byron Barton. p. cm. Summary: While three bears are away from home, Goldilocks ventures inside their house, tastes their porridge, tries their chairs, and finally falls asleep in Baby Bear's bed. ISBN 0-06-020423-0. — ISBN 0-06-020424-9 (lib. bdg.) (1. Bears—Folklore. 2. Folklore.) I. Goldilocks and the three bears. English. II. Title. PZ8.1.B3135 Th 1991 398.24'52974446—dc20 (E) 90-43151 CIP AC
4 5 6 7 8 9 10

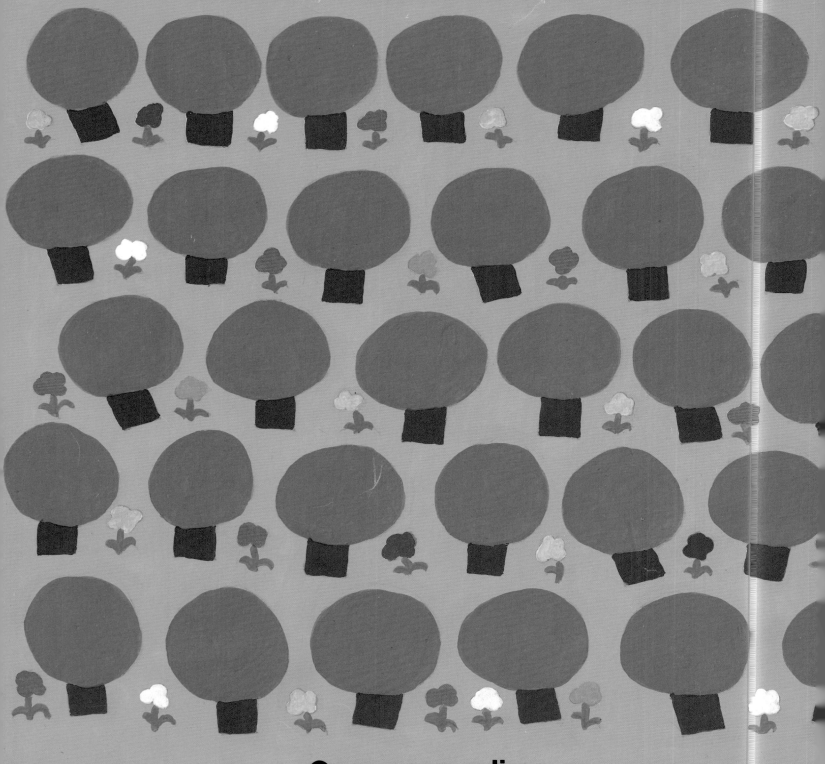

Once upon a time

there were three bears.

There was a Papa Bear

and a Mama Bear

and a Baby Bear.

One day Mama Bear
made some hot porridge.

She made a big bowl
for Papa Bear.

A medium-size bowl
for Mama Bear.

And a small bowl
for Baby Bear.

The porridge was very hot.

So the three bears went for a walk until it got cool.

Just then, along came a little girl named Goldilocks.

Goldilocks looked inside the house.
There she saw the three bowls of porridge.

Goldilocks was hungry,
so she tasted Papa Bear's porridge.
But it was too hot.

Then she tried Mama Bear's porridge.
But it was too cold.

Then she tried Baby Bear's porridge.
It was just right.

So she ate and ate until she ate it all.

Then Goldilocks wanted to sit down.
First she sat in Papa Bear's rocker.
But it rocked too fast.

Then she sat in Mama Bear's rocker.
It rocked too slow.

Then she sat in Baby Bear's rocker.
It rocked just right.

So Goldilocks rocked and rocked.
She rocked so much, the little rocker broke.

Then Goldilocks wanted to lie down.
First she tried Papa Bear's bed.
It was too hard.

Then she tried Mama Bear's bed.
It was too soft.

Then she tried Baby Bear's bed.
It was just right.

So Goldilocks fell asleep in Baby Bear's bed.

A little while later, the three bears came home.

The bears looked at their porridge, and Papa Bear said, "Someone has been eating my porridge."

Then Mama Bear said, "Someone has been eating my porridge."

And Baby Bear said, "Someone has been eating my porridge too, and now it is all gone."

Then the bears looked at their chairs,
and Papa Bear said,
"Someone has been sitting in my chair."

Then Mama Bear said, "Someone has been sitting in my chair."

And Baby Bear said, "Someone has been sitting in my chair too, and now it is broken in pieces."

Then the bears looked at their beds,
and Papa Bear said,
"Someone has been sleeping in my bed."

**And Mama Bear said,
"Someone has been sleeping in my bed."**

Then Baby Bear cried out,

When Goldilocks saw the three bears,

she jumped out of Baby Bear's bed and ran.

She ran and ran as fast as she could,

away from the three bears' house.

And the three bears never saw little Goldilocks again.